To Mia,

Wishing you a Merry
Christmas.
~Catie Cordero

The Magic Snow Globe

Written by Catie Cordero

Illustrated by Catie Cordero and Cindy Overbeek

FLYWHEEL
BOOKS

The Magic Snow Globe

Published by Flywheel Books, Zeeland, MI. *www.catiecordero.com*

Printed through CreateSpace, Charleston, SC.

Summary: Join the twins, Willow and Wendell Potter on an adventure that will reveal the secret to real Christmas magic.

ISBN-13: 978-1976057076

Dedication

To my family. You are my greatest Christmas blessing.

Acknowledgements

Many thanks to my husband, Jonathan, my biggest fan and supporter. I love you like crazy.

Thank you to my children for inspiring me with your wonder and imagination.

Thank you to my parents, Brian and Cindy, who've been cheering me on as a writer since I entered young authors in 6th grade! Also, without the help of my mother the illustrations in this book wouldn't be complete. Her expertise in painting brings each picture to life. I couldn't do it without you, Mom. Thanks for everything.

A special thank you to my sister, Carmen, for always encouraging me to write children's books. Okay sis, I'm doing it.

Thank you to my writing critique partners, Janna, Connie, Jonathan and Cindy for always believing in me and helping me refine my ideas.

And to all my other family members and friends, thank you for all your love, support and prayers in this journey. There are many names I'd like to state but this book can't contain them all.

Last but far from least, thank you God for sitting with me each day as we write together, dream together, and imagine the possibilities. I love you.

It was three days 'til Christmas.
The streets swarmed with bustle.
Shoppers rushed to buy gifts,
And the twins joined the hustle.

Willow and Wendell Potter,
Trailed their mom from shop to shop.
They walked along the snowy streets,
Tired and ready to drop.

Then they passed a small store,
Displaying items far from new.
Its storefront said antiques.
To the window Willow drew.

A single ray of light shone,
Through the frosted pane of glass.
It lit upon a snow globe,
With a base made of brass.

Willow tapped her brother.
"See that globe, isn't it grand?"
Wendell shrugged a shoulder.
"Too me it looks quite bland."

Mother said, "You may go in."
Willow raced ahead with glee.
She searched the shelves to find it,
Then the snow globe, she did see.

It contained a tree, full and tall.
Around it flew three fairies.
They strung a garland on it,
Made of snowflakes and red berries.

The tree had real pine needles.
The fairies' wings sparkled gold.
Wendell read the label.
It said, The Magic Globe.

They pooled their allowance,
Paying cash for their treasure.
Inside their shared bedroom,
They placed it on a dresser.

That night the twins lay snug,
About to doze off to sleep,
When a silver bell chimed,
Causing their hearts to leap.

Snow swirled 'round the globe,
In a flurry of white.
They jumped from their beds,
Stunned by the stark light.

Their hands reached out quick,
Fingers touching the glass.
A cold breeze swept through,
Transporting them in a flash.

"Welcome to Fairy Forest.
We're glad that you are here.
We could use your help,
With Christmas so near."

The twins gladly assisted,
Stringing garland overhead.
They made berry wreaths,
Fresh pies, and sweet bread.

Wendell folded his arms,
As he studied the tree.
"Where are all the presents?"
He asked curiously.

"Our gifts don't need wrapping,
For they are people we recall.
Our dear friends and family,
And a God who made them all."

The twins awoke in wonder,
Safely back in their beds.
Did last night really happen,
Or was it all in their heads?

They looked at the snow globe.
Their eyes widened in awe.
Now it held a toy soldier,
Sewing a puppy's paw.

That night, the twins waited,
Unable to rest.
When the silver bell rang,
They prepared for a new quest.

In a flicker, they traveled,
To the next magical land.
A toy soldier greeted them,
With a doll in his hand.

"Welcome to our factory.
Here we mend toys old or broken.
We make sure to fix them good.
So that each one can be chosen."

"New doesn't equal better.
Each toy deserves a home,
Together with a child,
So no one is alone."

Late on Christmas Eve,
The twins traveled once more.
They cheered with excitement,
For the land they'd explore.

They arrived at a stable.
It looked dingy and small.
Their hearts sank a little.
This place seemed a bit dull.

A cow mooed a welcome,
And a pony whispered, "Neigh."
They came upon a manger,
Where a special baby lay.

A sheep baaed, "This baby,
Will help everyone on earth.
That's why on this midnight,
We're celebrating his birth."

The twins stared speechless.
They never expected to meet,
A baby named Jesus.
They humbly bowed at his feet.

At last, it was the big day.
Christmas morning had arrived.
Willow and Wendell smiled,
With their parents at their side.

The Magic Globe had helped them,
Learn more about this season.
What they once had thought,
Was not at all the reason.

Christmas should remind us,
To give kindness and love.
To treasure every moment,
And thank the Lord above.

MERRY CHRISTMAS

Made in the USA
Lexington, KY
28 October 2017